You're Alone on the Deck of a Very Strange Ship . . .

You go below, calling out time after time. But there is never any answer. Occasionally a rat scuttles across your path.

In the captain's quarters, the log book is open.

> *August 23, 1873: We tried again to round the Cape of Good Hope. Storms fearsome. We fail again. . . .*
> *October 23, 1873: I am the last one left. Plague has taken us all. But the ship sails itself now, still trying to round the Cape.*

Slowly it dawns on you: you are on a ghost ship!

It you decide to return to your rowboat, turn to page 72.

If you decide to stay on board, turn to page 75.

REMEMBER:
THE NEXT MOVE IS UP TO YOU!

WHICH WAY BOOKS for you to enjoy

Available from ARCHWAY paperbacks

WHICH WAY BOOKS #7

CURSE OF THE SUNKEN TREASURE

R.G. Austin

ILLUSTRATED BY LORNA TOMEI

AN ARCHWAY PAPERBACK
Published by POCKET BOOKS • NEW YORK

AN ARCHWAY PAPERBACK *Original*

An Archway Paperback published by
POCKET BOOKS, a division of Simon & Schuster, Inc.
1230 Avenue of the Americas, New York, N.Y. 10020

Text Copyright © 1982 by R.G. Austin
Illustrations Copyright © 1982 by Simon & Schuster, Inc.

ISBN: 0-671-60109-1

First Archway Paperback printing June, 1982

10 9 8 7 6 5

AN ARCHWAY PAPERBACK and colophon are
registered trademarks of Simon & Schuster, Inc.

WHICH WAY is a registered trademark
of Simon & Schuster, Inc.

Printed in the U.S.A.

IL3+

For my goddaughters,
Kathy and Patricia

Attention!

Which Way Books must be read in a special way. DO NOT READ THE PAGES IN ORDER. If you do, the story will make no sense at all. Instead, follow the directions at the bottom of each page until you come to an ending. Only then should you return to the beginning and start over again, making different choices this time.

There are many possibilities for exciting adventures. Some of the endings are good; some of the endings are bad. If you meet a terrible fate, you can reverse it in your next story by making new choices.

Remember: Follow the directions carefully, and have fun!

You are sound asleep, but your mind whirls with restless and disturbing dreams. Suddenly you wake up. Your room is filled with an unearthly green glow that shines through the window. Eerie shadows hover around you.

You are seized by a compelling need to discover the source of the green light. You get out of bed, put on your clothes, and walk outside.

You live in a small fishing village, and a shimmering beam of green light is coming from somewhere offshore. You climb into a boat and begin to row. Soon you are enveloped in a thick green fog. You cannot see where you are going; all you know is that you must continue to follow the light.

(continued on page 3)

Suddenly a ship looms before you. Its huge masts rise out of the fog and its white sails, flapping in the wind, are bathed in a deep, vibrant green glow. A ladder hangs over the side of the ship.

You row to the ladder, climb up it, and step onto the deck of the ship.

"Welcome aboard," says a man with a white beard and a pipe in his mouth. "I am Captain Abel. Hurry, we must sail with the high tide. There is little time left.

"We are about to set out on a strange and dangerous journey," the captain says. "If you do not wish to go, please leave the ship now."

(continued on page 4)

You look around. There is only one other person on board, a strange-looking man who is standing off to one side. You decide to stay.

"Hundreds of years ago," the captain continues, "a glowing green diamond, the size of a basketball, broke off from Planet Galinka and plunged through space to Earth. Many people have possessed the diamond and they have all met untimely deaths.

"The last people to steal the diamond were pirates. The pirates, the diamond, and two million dollars' worth of gold sank to the bottom of the ocean when their ship hit a glacier.

"On rare nights the glow from the diamond is reflected upward from the bottom of the ocean. That is the source of the green light. It is my intention to follow the light and find the treasure."

(continued on page 5)

You cannot resist the lure of searching for sunken treasure and you agree to go.

Soon you are sailing in the dark through open sea.

"They don't want us to find the diamond," says a voice behind you. You turn and see the strange-looking man.

"What do you mean?" you ask.

"The beings from Planet Galinka have put a curse on anyone who searches for the diamond. Captain Abel is crazy, you know." Then the man whispers, "My name is Stix, and I have a plan. Come with me and I'll tell you."

If you go with Stix, turn to page 10.

If you stay with the captain, turn to page 17.

After dinner, you and the captain sit on the deck of the ship. The sky is velvet black and the stars are golden lights above you.

The captain plays his guitar and gives you a flute. You are amazed at the beautiful music you are able to play. The music blends with the beauty of the night. The world is peaceful and kind and gentle.

If you decide to sleep on deck, turn to page 13.

If you decide to sleep in your cabin, turn to page 19.

You climb through the door and it closes behind you. You are frightened, but you are also relieved that Stix has refused to come with you.

There are three aliens inside the saucer.

"Why did you come here?" the leader asks.

You are afraid that if you tell him you are looking for the green diamond, he will kill you. But you are also afraid to lie.

If you say that your ship sank and that you took refuge in a lifeboat, turn to page 11.

If you tell the truth, turn to page 26.

You put on your wet suit and scuba tank and dive into the water. The green light illuminates your way.

When you reach the bottom, you are awed by the size of the green diamond nestled in the middle of an icy glacier. Nearby, the hull of an old ship protrudes through the ice.

(continued on page 9)

Carefully, you wiggle your way into the hull. There, sitting on a massive treasure chest, is Stix. He is holding a knife in his hand.

If you confront Stix, turn to page 12.

If you surface to tell the captain, turn to page 21.

The man tells you his plan.

The next night you and Stix lower the lifeboat, climb down the ladder, and row away.

The green light seems brighter as you row toward it. But it disappears at dawn.

"Where do we go now?" you ask.

"We don't go anywhere. We wait," says Stix.

"For what?"

"For *them*," he says, pulling a pistol from his pocket and pointing it at you. "Don't move."

You have no choice.
Turn to page 15.

"Our ship sank, and we are lost at sea in the lifeboat," you say.

"You do not seem to understand the meaning of truth," the alien says. "We cannot work with someone who is so confused. It is a pity.

"We wished to consult with a human about the green diamond. But obviously we have made an error in choosing you. We have no choice: we will sail close to shore so that you can return home. Your life will always be ordinary, without adventure, and without challenge. That is now your fate."

The End

You indicate that you will help Stix carry the treasure to the surface. Stix nods; he knows that there is no way he can get the treasure up by himself.

Together you manage to raise the chest. The captain helps you attach a pully to the chest and hoist it onto the deck.

"What about the diamond?" you ask.

"No way," says Stix. "It's cursed."

The captain nods in agreement. "Two million dollars in gold ought to do us just fine."

Jubilant, you, Captain Abel, and Stix celebrate. Then you set sail for home.

When you are three days away from home, you see a ship on the horizon. When it gets closer, you discover that it is flying the Jolly Roger pirate flag.

If you sail directly west, turn to page 30.

If you try to outsail the pirates, turn to page 39.

The night is so inviting that you decide to sleep on deck. Wrapped in a sleeping bag, you gaze at the stars.

You blink your eyes when you see red and green stars. They fade in and out, and you are not certain that they are anything significant.

If you grow sleepy and close your eyes, turn to page 25.

If you call the captain, turn to page 29.

You travel northwest for three days. On the morning of the fourth day the green light vanishes.

You are wondering what to do when the captain cries, "Land ho!"

You jump up, excited. Out of the mist on the horizon a mountain thrusts out of the sea. The captain turns the ship toward land, and soon you are anchored in a cove.

Captain Abel asks you to take the small rowboat and see if there is food and water on shore.

You row to the island, pull the boat up on the beach and walk into the forest toward the sound of a waterfall. You are filled with an extraordinary sense of peace as you walk, as if you have entered a new world.

You come to the waterfall and behind it there is a small opening in the rocks. You are compelled to go through the opening.

Turn to page 22.

"Why are you doing this?" you ask. "I've done you no harm."

"Nor will you," Stix says. "Because when the beings arrive from Planet Galinka, you will be my hostage."

Throughout the day you watch the sky, waiting for a flying saucer to appear. But nothing happens.

"Perhaps they are not coming today," Stix says.

You breathe a sigh of relief. Neither of you sees the circle of glowing green water moving toward you.

Suddenly the water boils and swirls, and a small green saucer emerges.

A door opens slowly, and a strange mechanical voice says, "Enter."

If you go into the alien ship, turn to page 7.

If you would rather take your chances with Stix, turn to page 24.

You sail northeast. Each day the green light grows brighter.

On the evening of the tenth day the captain informs you that the ship is anchored directly over the treasure. A green light beams up at you from the ocean bottom.

If you want to dive now, turn to page 8.

If you think it would be better to wait until morning, turn to page 6.

You look at Stix. His eyes glow red in the dim light, and you do not like his expression at all.

"I think I'll stay with the captain," you say as politely as you can.

"Your mistake, my friend," Stix says. "You'll be sorry. I'm getting off this ship right now."

The ship sets sail toward the green light.

At dawn on the second day you are standing with the captain at the helm when you both notice that the green light seems to split and go off in two directions.

Captain Abel says to you, "Which way do you think we should go?"

If you think you should travel northwest, turn to page 14.

If you think you should travel northeast, turn to page 16.

You are drifting to sleep when you hear strange music. Then, to your amazement, the ship starts to move. You call to the captain and both of you rush up on deck.

You are astounded to see that the ship is being pushed at an amazing speed through the water by five blue whales. You can hear their strange, otherworldly music coming from the water. You think they are communicating with each other. But then you hear an answering music coming from above your head.

You look up and see a flying saucer hovering above the ship.

If you decide that there is nothing you can do except wait, turn to page 31.

If you try to join the conversation by playing your flute, turn to page 36.

Furiously, you try to row away from the saucer.

"Stop!" Stix yells. But it is too late. The aliens, angry at your lack of cooperation, blast you with a laser.

The End

You swim to the surface and breathlessly tell the captain what has happened.

"He has as much right to the treasure as we have, but threatening you with a knife is a criminal act," says the captain.

"His boat must be hidden behind that glacial peak," he adds.

"Sooner or later he'll run out of air in his tank," you say.

"Maybe we should be waiting for him when he returns to his boat," the captain suggests.

If you try to devise an alternate plan, turn to page 35.

If you go to Stix's boat, turn to page 46.

You step into a dark cave. A thin shaft of light shines from the other end.

You crawl out into the light and are startled by a voice.

(continued on page 23)

"How did you get here?" says a woman dressed in a long, flowing gown.

"Who are you?" you ask.

"I am Fantasia, your guide," she answers. "Would you like to visit Estrella, a land of perfection? Or would you rather visit Terra, a land of human error and imperfection?"

If you choose Estrella, turn to page 53.

If you choose Terra, turn to page 64.

"Come out so we can see you," you call to the aliens.

"We cannot do that," the mechanical voice says. "You must enter the saucer."

"You gotta be kidding," you answer, and you grab the oars and start to row away.

"You're crazy!" yells Stix. "They'll zap us."

"At least this way we've got a chance," you say.

You row furiously; your boat sails through the water at an incredible speed. But when you stop to rest for a moment, the boat continues to move, and you realize that you are not in control. Your speed and your direction are being manipulated by the alien spacecraft, which is beneath you near the ocean bottom. You are frightened.

If you try to row in the other direction, turn to page 20.

If you stop rowing and allow the saucer to guide you, turn to page 28.

You are drifting into sleep when you hear a strange musical sound. You open your eyes and are horrified to see a beam of light shining directly on you from a saucer that is hovering over the ship.

You feel a strange pull and then you are moving up into the saucer, enclosed in a beam of light.

If you try to negotiate with the aliens, turn to page 50.

If you argue with the aliens, turn to page 57.

"I was looking for the source of the green light," you say, frightened at what the aliens will do.

"Why do you wish to find it?"

"Because of the treasure."

"You have been honest with us," the leader says. "Others have lied. We know now that we can trust you with our mission."

The leader then explains, "We are inhabitants of Planet Galinka. The green diamond is our beacon, our navigational guide in the galaxy. But now the light has grown dim. For many years the diamond has lain protected in an underwater glacial valley.

(continued on page 27)

"We must inspect the diamond, but we cannot do it by ourselves. If we leave our ship, we will disintegrate in Earth's atmosphere. That is why we need a human to dive down and bring us the diamond."

The alien pauses. "Will you help us?" he asks.

If your answer is yes, *turn to page 34.*

If your answer is no, *turn to page 40.*

You settle in for the ride as the saucer guides you through the water at the speed of sound. You whiz past entire continents as if they were miniatures.

You have been traveling for more than an hour when Stix points to the sky and yells, "Look!"

Above you, a gigantic spaceship hovers; its lights blink in erratic patterns. Without warning, the saucer surfaces and blinks back. Then the saucer rises in the air and disappears into the mother ship.

You are left stranded with Stix. A heavy fog rolls in, and you hear the eerie sound of a foghorn nearby.

Within minutes, a huge form looms in the distance. Soon you can see that it is a two-masted schooner.

If you row toward the schooner, turn to page 44.

If you are fearful of the ghostly appearance of the schooner and try to avoid it, turn to page 48.

You go below and wake up the captain.

"There's something weird in the sky," you tell him. "I think you'd better come have a look."

You walk up on deck and look at the sky. At first you see nothing. Then the red and green lights flash again.

"There!" you say, pointing. When the captain looks up, the lights are gone.

"You must be imagining things," Captain Abel says. "I'm going back to sleep."

After he is gone, you see the lights again; this time they are more distinct.

If you wait to see if the lights stay in the sky, turn to page 43.

If you go wake up the captain again, turn to page 52.

You sail west, directly into the sun. You cannot see because the sun is shining into your eyes; but you know that the pirates, too, will be blinded by the sun. After a few minutes, they abandon the chase.

You have escaped. You set sail in the direction of home, your heart filled with joy and the treasure chest filled with gold.

The End

If you are not ready to go home and you would like to go ashore and explore a cave, turn to page 22.

You and Captain Abel are transfixed by what is happening. The ship has never moved through the water at such speed, yet it is an oddly peaceful ride.

The saucer and the whales continue their haunting and unforgettable music.

After about an hour, the ship comes to a halt. The saucer dips first to one side and then to the other; then it disappears into the sky.

The whales, with one last flip of their gigantic tails, dive into the darkest depths of the ocean. You are alone once more.

You understand now that you must not seek the treasure, that somehow it is important for it to remain undisturbed by human beings. You smile, sad that the treasure will not be yours, but thrilled by the extraordinary experience that you will never forget.

The End

"I think we should bring up the diamond," the captain says. "It's probably more valuable than the gold."

"Stix told me there's a curse on the diamond," you say.

"Nonsense!" says Captain Abel. "There's no such thing as a curse."

Together you dive down into the water. The captain grabs the diamond and swims to the surface.

Then you stand with Captain Abel on the deck of the ship and admire the beauty of the splendid stone you have brought up from the bottom of the sea. Visions of being super rich dance in your head.

(continued on page 33)

Suddenly a gigantic shadow falls over you. You look up and see a small flying saucer hovering in the air overhead. A strange-sounding voice calls out, "Return the diamond to the ice cavern immediately."

If you return the diamond, turn to page 54.

If you refuse to return it, turn to page 59.

"Yes," you say, with hesitation. "I'd be glad to help."

"Good," says the alien. "Here is a kylon membrane that will cover your body, protect you from the cold, and enable you to breathe under the water. When we are above the diamond, you will dive down and bring it back to us."

In minutes the leader says, "We're here. It is time for your work."

"But we haven't moved," you say.

"Oh, yes," the leader says. "We travel at the speed of sound. The water slows us down, you see."

You swim out into the icy water, but you do not even feel the cold. You dive straight down toward the green light.

Suddenly a shadowy form passes over you. You look up and see that the shadow is a giant sea serpent.

If you hurry back to the saucer, turn to page 47.

If you continue to swim in the same direction, turn to page 51.

You and the captain take a rowboat and wait directly above the green diamond. You watch the water for the bubbles that will signal the fact that Stix is surfacing.

You are waiting when he emerges from the water with the green diamond in his hands.

"Sorry to disappoint you," the captain says, pointing a gun at Stix. "Come along. You belong in the brig."

Furious, Stix drops the diamond back into the water.

With Stix locked in the ship's jail, you and the captain confer about what to do next.

If you decide to wait until morning and then go after the treasure, turn to page 6.

If you attempt to bring up the diamond now, turn to page 32.

You pick up your flute and begin to play. Suddenly the music of the whales stops. Then the alien music stops. It is your turn.

You play the most haunting, lyrical tune that you know, trying to tell them through music that they have nothing to fear, that you will not disturb their treasure without permission.

You stop playing. Then the whales begin their song. And, when the whales stop, the saucer picks up the melody. Back and forth, the music is traded, the songs are sung.

(continued on page 37)

Finally, the last note drifts on the crimson dawn sky. The whales, with a huge surge, dive into the black ocean waters.

A beam of light slowly emerges from the saucer. In its glow you can see an additional green light caught in the beam. It descends onto the deck of the ship.

It is a piece of green diamond, sparkling in the morning sun, a gift from the aliens to you.

With one last haunting melody, the saucer spins away and disappears in the light.

The End

If you have not had enough excitement and would like to follow the green light again, turn to page 14.

You raise all the sails and pick up speed. But the pirate ship is faster, and soon it is alongside you.

Before you can do anything, three pirates have boarded your ship, all of them brandishing swords.

"Your money or your life," says the leader of the pirates.

If you show the pirates where the treasure chest is hidden, turn to page 42.

If you do not reveal its presence, turn to page 58.

"I would like to help you, but I do not know how to swim," you say.

"That is bad," says the leader. "Until we have repaired the problem of the light, you must stay with us as our guest. We cannot risk your returning to your people and telling them about us."

If you try to convince the aliens that they should let you go, turn to page 56.

If you agree to go with the aliens, turn to page 62.

You walk up to the helm. The wheel is moving, but there is nobody standing next to it. During the next few hours, sails are raised and lowered, doors slam, stairs creak. But no one is there except you. *The ship is being sailed by ghosts.*

For days you stay on the ship. After a while you even become used to living with ghosts.

One night a fearsome storm blows in from the west. You are tossed and turned.

You take refuge in the captain's quarters, hoping that the boat, guided by ghosts, can manage to ride out the storm.

You know you will go mad if you don't get off this ship soon. You realize then that you will have to take the helm and try your best to set sail on a new course.

You have no choice.
Turn to page 75.

Reluctantly, you show the pirates the treasure chest. They transfer it to their ship and then set sail.

You are sad that you have lost the treasure, but you are grateful that you had such a wonderful adventure.

The End

You wait, your eyes focused on the sky. You feel no fear. Instead, you are overcome with a sense of joy and anticipation. You are not disappointed.

Soon the red lights become more and more distinct. Then they are spinning in a circle over your head. It is only then that you realize that you are looking at a flying saucer!

A green beam of light suddenly shines down on you.

You cannot move.

*You have no choice.
Turn to page 61.*

You row toward the ship while Stix waves his shirt and calls out.

When you are close to the ship, you notice that there is a cargo net draped over the side.

"Hold the lifeboat while I grab the net!" Stix yells.

You maneuver the lifeboat into position. Stix grabs the net. Then he shoves you away with his foot.

"Hey!" you yell. "I want to climb aboard, too!"

"Tough break!" Stix says with a sardonic laugh. Your boat drifts close to the ship once more and Stix kicks you away. But this time, he loses his footing and falls into the water.

You row frantically toward him, but before you can help him, he is surrounded by a dozen shark fins. Then he disappears.

(continued on page 45)

You row sadly back to the schooner, grab hold of the cargo net, and climb aboard the ship.

"Hello!" you yell. But there is not a sound on the boat.

If you check the helm, turn to page 41.

If you go below, turn to page 63.

You row to Stix's boat with the captain. Then you wait. After three hours, you know that something has happened.

You dive down into the ice cavern. Stix is gone and so is the treasure. When you swim to the surface, you tell the captain.

"We've been sitting in a decoy boat," says the captain. "We didn't think about all the alternatives, and now we have lost the treasure."

The End

You start to swim back toward the saucer as fast as you can. The serpent waves its tail wildly in the water. Its head moves close enough so that you can see its red eyes. Then its mouth opens. Its enormous teeth shine green in the light.

Closer and closer the mouth comes until it closes over you.

The End

The fog becomes so thick that you can barely see your hands.

"Stix," you call, "are you there?"

There is no answer. You reach over to poke him, but he is gone. You are frightened. You listen to the foghorn. Instead of repeating the same sounds over and over again, the sounds vary. You listen carefully and jot down the pattern on a pad you are carrying in your pocket. You use dashes for the long sounds of the foghorn and dots for the short sounds.

(continued on page 49)

Foghorn Message

```
. . .    —      . .    . . .   .   . . .
— _      .    . _     _ .   . . .
— . .    .    . _    _     . . . .
```

Before you decipher the message, decide whether you wish to row closer to the foghorn or away from it. After you decide, use the key to the code on page 113 to figure out the message. When you have deciphered the message, you will know your fate.

The End

"Why are you doing this?" you ask.

"We must protect our green diamond," an alien answers in a mechanical voice.

"What about the gold?" you ask.

"Gold? We care nothing for gold," the alien says. "It is of no use to us."

"If we leave the green diamond, may we take the gold?" you ask.

"Of course. As I said, the gold means nothing."

You smile, jubilant that soon you will be the owner of a real pirate's treasure.

The End

You swim frantically toward the green light. The water grows turbulent around you, and you know that the serpent is gaining on you.

As you swim closer to the light, you discover that the light is shining through a crack in the glacier. The crack is at the top of a huge ice cavern.

You give one final kick toward the crack as the monster lunges for you, his mouth open wide.

Turn to page 66.

You run below and wake up the captain, telling him that you see the lights again.

"Now you're really getting silly," the captain says. "Try to put some reins on your overactive imagination."

Captain Abel speaks with such forcefulness and authority that you believe him. You climb into your bed and go to sleep.

When you awaken in the morning, you hear familiar noises. You run up on deck and are astounded to discover that, while you were sleeping, the ship was transported back to the harbor of the fishing village where you live.

You know then that it would have been wiser to follow your own mind instead of somebody else's. You wonder if you missed the adventure of a lifetime because you did not have the courage of your own conviction.

The End

"I would like to visit perfection, of course," you answer. "Isn't that what everyone would want?"

Fantasia smiles, then she leads you along a green mossy path that borders a brook. You cross an arched wooden bridge and enter a small town.

You look around and realize that everyone here is beautiful. The men are the most handsome you have ever seen. The women are the most beautiful. The children say *please* and *thank you* without being prompted; and the birds sing only when they are asked. Everyone, without exception, smiles and laughs.

There is a carnival in progress and you ask if you might play some of the games.

"Of course," Fantasia says.

If you want to play the wheel of fortune, turn to page 68.

If you want to throw darts at a target, turn to page 73.

"Of course we will return the diamond," you say, "but what about the gold?"

"Gold? We do not care for gold. It is the diamond that is valuable to us. It is one of our navigational guides in the galaxy."

You dive down to the ice cavern and put the diamond back in place. Then you struggle with the captain to raise the chest of gold to the surface. Finally, with the aid of a pulley, you hoist the chest on deck.

You try to break the lock with a hammer; then you try to pry it open with a crowbar. Nothing works.

You notice that the decoration on the top of the chest is a strange arrangement of dots and lines. You suspect that this might be a code that reveals the combination for the lock.

(continued on page 55)

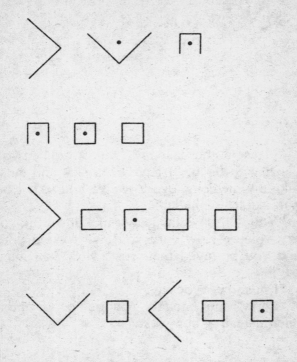

If you can decipher the code, the chest of gold is yours.

The End

Note: Turn to page 114 for the key to the code.

"Please do not take me," you say. Then you plead with them. "I have been sick and must take my medicine every twelve hours. If I do not take it, I will die."

"You lie!" says the leader in a powerful, angry voice. "How dare you! We trusted you, and you betrayed that trust. Now you must pay!"

"I'm sorry," you say.

"Sorry is not enough. You are now our prisoner instead of our guest."

The End

"You can't do this to me!" you scream. "I didn't do anything! Let me out of the light!"

"If you cooperate, we will not harm you," a mechanical voice says.

"Cooperate! How can I cooperate when you kidnap me in a beam of light!" you scream.

Zap!

The End

"We have no treasure," you say.

"Then it's your life," the pirate says.

"Wait!" says Stix. "I'll show you the treasure chest if you'll allow me to join you."

You are furious as you watch Stix reveal the hidden location of the chest. Although it is heavy, the three pirates manage to transfer it to their ship. Just as Stix is about to jump over to their ship, the pirates shove him backwards onto your deck. Then they sail away.

"You're a traitor, Stix," says Captain Abel. "You'll pay for this."

The End

"We did not take the diamond from an alien planet," you say. "If we did, it would belong to you. This diamond was right here on Planet Earth. Therefore, it belongs to human beings."

"And that means us," the captain adds.

"Then there *is* no more 'us,' " the voice says. A laser gun slowly emerges from the saucer. You do not even hear a click.

The End

You feel yourself being lifted off the deck of the ship into the saucer. When you are inside, you are surrounded by prism-covered aliens.

"What are you doing?" you ask.

"Do not fear. We mean you no harm. In one minute we will put you back on your boat," an alien says.

"You must tell the captain in the morning that what you saw was your imagination—that there were no strange lights in the sky.

"You must also convince him not to disturb the diamond. Take the gold. It is yours. But leave the diamond alone. You must never reveal to anyone that you saw us."

You nod in agreement, sad that you will never be able to tell about the aliens, but happy that you are the only person on Earth who has ever talked with the aliens from Planet Galinka.

The End

You feel a sudden movement of the saucer as it breaks through the surface of the water with a roar and surges into the sky. You look up through the porthole in the ceiling. Far out in space you see whirling red and green lights.

"That is our mother ship," the leader says.

In seconds your saucer spins through an open door on the underside of the mother ship. Then the gigantic door slides closed.

"Come," says the leader. "I must take you to the Great Master."

You step outside the saucer into the mother ship and suddenly a laser beam of red light flashes past you.

"We have been infiltrated by the enemy," says the leader. "Quick! Come with me."

"No!" says another alien, grabbing you by the hand. "Come with me. I will protect you."

If you go with the leader, turn to page 65.

If you go with the other alien, turn to page 70.

You go below, calling out time after time. But there is never any answer. Occasionally a rat scuttles across your path.

In the captain's quarters, the log book is open.

> *August 23, 1873: We tried again to round the Cape of Good Hope. Storms fearsome. We fail again.*
>
> *August 24, 1873: Again no luck in rounding the Cape.*
>
> *September 4, 1873: Failure! I vow that I will round the Cape if it takes me an eternity!*

The log stops here, except for one final entry written in a different hand.

> *October 23, 1873: I am the last one left. Plague has taken us all. But the ship sails itself now, still trying to round the Cape.*

Slowly it dawns on you: you are on a ghost ship!

If you decide to return to your rowboat, turn to page 72.

If you decide to stay on board, turn to page 75.

You travel with Fantasia over a steep, rocky path. You are caught in a sudden rainstorm and you can barely see ahead of you.

Cold and shivering, you continue to climb. Just as you reach the highest point of your journey, the storm abates and the sun peeks through the clouds. On the horizon a rainbow arches over the valley below you. It is an awesome sight.

In the distance you see a cabin with smoke coming out of the chimney. Below you is a town.

If you want to warm yourself by the fire in the cabin, turn to page 69.

If you would rather go into town, turn to page 74.

The leader takes your hand and pulls you into the saucer. "With luck," he says, "the lasers will hit the mechanism that controls the doors. If that happens, we will make our escape."

Terrified, you wait as red and green lasers flash around the saucer. Then the giant doors slide open.

"This is our chance," says the leader.

The saucer glides quickly out of the mother ship. Just as you think you are safe, a laser zaps through the porthole and the leader falls unconscious to the floor.

The ship spins crazily, and you know that you must bring it under control. On the panel where the leader was standing there are two levers, a silver one and a gold one.

If you push the silver lever, turn to page 77.

If you push the gold lever, turn to page 88.

You squeeze through the crevice; the monster is too big to follow. You find yourself in an enormous underground ice cavern of awesome and unearthly beauty. In the middle of the cavern the green diamond shines like a beacon.

You realize that the dimming of the diamond has been caused by centuries of ice narrowing the entrance to the cave, thus preventing the light from escaping.

As you swim toward the diamond, you see the outline of a pirate ship beneath the ice; its hull is protruding into the cave.

(continued on page 67)

Suddenly there is a crash as loud as a thousand thunders. The serpent is banging its head against the sides of the opening. You fear he will soon break through and be able to enter the cave.

On the side of the cave is another opening that leads into a tunnel.

If you try to escape from the serpent by going into the tunnel, turn to page 81.

If you remain in the cave, turn to page 89.

The man who runs the wheel of fortune welcomes you with a broad grin. You give him a coin and bet on number 63. The wheel spins, then stops.

"I won!" you shriek with glee as the man gives you a small pocketknife for a prize.

Again and again you try, and each time you win. The tenth time you win you are not quite so joyful. The fifteenth time you are bored.

"Do I always win?" you ask.

"Of course," Fantasia says, smiling. "That's perfection."

"Then I don't want it," you say. "I would rather experience some risk and adventure in my life."

"As you wish," Fantasia says. "Come with me."

Turn to page 64.

You walk with Fantasia to the cabin and knock on the door.

"What d'ya want?" a woman says when she opens the door.

"We got caught in the storm," you answer. "We're cold and need to dry ourselves by a fire."

"This ain't a hotel, it's a private home," the woman says, and she slams the door in your face.

"I guess we'd better go on to town," you tell your guide.

Turn to page 74.

"Follow me!" cries the alien.

You run behind him to the center of the mother ship. There, a hydraulic air elevator is standing with its door open.

"We have to get to the control room," the alien says.

You step into the round laserproof glass elevator and are lifted on pockets of air to the top of the ship. The door opens, and you enter the control room. The Great Master turns to look at you.

"What's happening down there?" the Great Master says.

"It's a mutiny," says the alien as he points his laser at the Master. "We're taking over the ship."

(continued on page 71)

"Everybody stay where you are," the alien says. "And that includes you, Earthling," he adds, pointing the laser gun directly at you.

If you do as the alien says, turn to page 79.

If you try to overpower the alien, turn to page 103.

Sadly, you climb down the cargo net and step into the boat. You detach the line that connects you to the ship.

Slowly, the distance between you widens. And soon you are alone on the open sea.

Just as you are about to pick up the oars, a huge wave breaks over you and washes the oars from the lifeboat.

Now you are not only alone, but you are also at the mercy of the sea. You can only hope that soon a ship or plane will spot you and come to your rescue.

The End

The first dart you throw hits the bull's-eye. Then the next and the next. At first you are thrilled, but you soon grow bored with winning all the time.

"What's the matter?" asks Fantasia.

"I get bored if I never lose. Challenge and risk are the things that make winning fun."

"What you need is a warm home-cooked meal and a good night's sleep," she says. "Come home with me."

It sounds tempting to you, for you are quite exhausted. But you wonder if you should do something more exciting.

If you go home with Fantasia, turn to page 76.

If you look for something else to do, turn to page 86.

By the time you reach town you are exhausted.

The streets are filled with a wonderful mixture of people. Their faces are ugly and beautiful, ordinary and unique. Some people scowl, others laugh and sing.

In the center of the town square two children are squabbling over who should divide a piece of cake.

"You always cut me the smallest," says the girl.

"But you do the same thing to me," says the boy, "so it's fair."

"No, it's not!"

If you ignore the children and continue on your tour, turn to page 80.

If you help the children solve their problem, turn to page 83.

For days you stay on the boat. Finally, you realize that the boat continues to try to round the Cape and always fails. You realize that you must sail the ship in a different direction if you are to save yourself.

You take the helm and guide the ship away from the Cape. Then, using the Southern Cross as a celestial navigation guide, you turn north.

On the eighth day you sight land. You do not know whether you should sail until you see a port or simply head the ship toward land.

If you head directly for land, turn to page 84.

If you wait for a port, turn to page 98.

Fantasia's home is beautiful. Not a thing is out of place. You are almost afraid to sit down.

Her three children are dressed in perfectly matching clothes. They are always polite and they never, ever fight.

For dinner you eat a perfectly balanced meal. And in the morning your breakfast is also perfect.

You accept Fantasia's invitation to stay for three days. Each dinner is the same as the one before. Each breakfast is the same. Each lunch is the same. Nothing changes, because it is all perfect.

It is also very, very boring.

You are grateful to leave on the fourth morning, even though you have been treated perfectly.

You are delighted when you return to the ship and the captain is waiting for you.

"I can't wait for something unexpected to happen," you say. "Let's set sail!"

Turn to page 16.

You push the silver lever. Suddenly the saucer stops spinning and moves with amazing speed away from the Earth and out into space.

I'm safe for the time being, you think. The ship moves effortlessly for over an hour. Then it slows down.

It is only then that you consider the purpose of a mother ship. *This saucer is not designed for extensive space travel,* you think.

Your thoughts are confirmed. The ship slows down and begins to float aimlessly in space.

You lean down and shake the leader.

"Wake up," you scream. "Wake up!"

The End

You pick up the red strip and lick it gingerly. It tastes like mashed potatoes, so you put it in your mouth and eat it.

"That nourishment aids in the growth of our skin," the Great Master explains.

You are appalled when you see small prisms beginning to form on your body.

The End

Terrified, you do not move.

Suddenly the door flies open. "Drop it!" says an armed officer.

The mutinous alien turns toward the door. "I may have lost," he says. "But I'll never let *you* win."

He aims his laser at the control panel and shoots. The last thing you know is that the ship is disintegrating.

The End

Fantasia begins to walk faster. "We must find shelter soon," she says.

"Why?" you ask.

"Werewolves, of course," Fantasia says. "Just last month we lost one of our children to a werewolf."

"I'm not afraid of them," you say. "There's no such thing as a werewolf. Where do you think they live?" you ask jokingly.

"In the forest," Fantasia says, pointing to the dark trees beyond.

If you want to prove there are no werewolves, turn to page 91.

If you want to seek shelter with Fantasia, turn to page 101.

You swim frantically toward the side tunnel, fearful you will not reach it before the serpent breaks into the room.

You swim into the tunnel. Light from the diamond shines dimly inside. You continue to swim as the crashes grow louder. Then there is an enormous roar that sounds like an explosion.

The light disappears and the tunnel is cut off from the cave. You are trapped.

The End

The guard grabs you roughly and takes you down a long corridor. You take a hydraulic air elevator that plunges you thousands of feet into the center of the planet.

At the bottom the guard shoves you toward a fence of lights. It flashes off temporarily in order for you to pass, then it turns on again.

You are surrounded by lights.

"You are imprisoned in lasers," the guard says. "If you try to pass through them, you will die." Then she leaves.

If you stay there quietly and wait to see what happens next, turn to page 93.

If you try to pass the lasers, turn to page 106.

"Here! Let me help," you say to the children.

"You cut it!" says one child.

"Then it's fair," says the other.

"No, it's not," you say. "Here's what I want you to do. *You* cut the cake," you tell the little girl. Just as the boy is about to protest, you say to him, "And you choose which piece you want."

The children are silent. Then the boy smiles. "That's fair," he says. The girl agrees.

Fantasia looks at you and smiles. "Thank you," she says. "You are very wise. You may remain in our land as long as you like."

The End

You head for land, fearful that the ship will crash onto the shore. Fortunately, you run a-ground on a sandbar. *Good,* you think. *I'll swim to shore from here and use the ship as shelter when I need it.*

On the beach, you look around. Suddenly you are surrounded by three burly men.

"Where're you going, mate?" one asks.

"Yeah, where?" asks the other, pulling a dagger from his belt and holding it to you.

You explain about the ghost ship.

"Well, ain't that a sad story," says one.

"Yeah, ain't it," says the other. "Well, I guess we can always use another hand at our work."

"What do you do?" you ask.

"Smuggle diamonds, of course. And that's what you do, too, if you know what's good for you."

The End

You run to the window. You are awed by the power of the quake. You watch as the chimney of the house next door begins to sway. With a loud crack, the chimney snaps. You are horrified to see that it is headed straight for you.

The End

You thank Fantasia and continue alone in the land of perfection.

You see a group of children sitting quietly in a park. You approach them and start to talk.

"Do you want to play hide-and-seek?"

"Of course not," says one of the children. "We might get dirty."

"Do you want to go swimming?" you ask.

"My hair will get wet," says a little girl.

You nod and then walk over to a dusty part of the park. You borrow a pail and fetch some water; then you pour the water into the dirt. Soon you have created a giant and wonderfully messy mud hole.

(continued on page 87)

At first the children are shocked. Then, one by one, they come over to you and start to play. Soon the entire group is covered with mud.

You and the children play joyously in the mud all afternoon.

When it is time for the children to go home, they all thank you for showing them how to have so much fun.

The End

You push the gold lever. The saucer stops spinning and begins to fall toward Earth. You do not know how to stop it. Then, to your relief, the saucer moves into orbit around Earth.

You are wondering how long you can stay in orbit when the alien leader opens his eyes.

"Good," he says. "We will stay in orbit until the battle is over. If we win, I will take you to your home before returning to the mother ship."

You smile with relief.

The End

You swim behind the hull of the ship.

You can see nothing, but the crashes grow louder. Suddenly the serpent breaks into the cave. It searches everywhere, swinging its long neck back and forth.

Then it spies you.

If you try to swim away, turn to page 100.

If you stay by the hull, turn to page 105.

You swing one more time, then you let go of the rope. You fly over the laser wall and land with a thud on the floor.

Just then the elevator door opens. The Great Master steps out of the door.

"How did you get out?" he asks.

"I used my Earthling brain," you reply.

"Then it is a better brain than we suspected," the Great Master says. "Because of that, we will release you so that we can make further studies."

"When the studies are over, will you send me back to prison?" you ask.

"Of course not. We have too much respect for brains to do that. When we complete our studies, I will take you back to Earth."

"Thank you," you say with a sigh of relief.

The End

You walk into the forest. The light of the moon shines through the trees. Deeper and deeper you go into the forest, confident you will not be harmed.

Soon it is past midnight and the moon is low, casting little light now on the path before you.

You hear movement. From the corner of your eye you see two tiny red lights. At first you do not know what they are. And then you realize, to your horror, that they are eyes.

If you try to hide, turn to page 104.

If you run back in the direction you came from, turn to page 109.

The green strip smells like onions and tastes like chocolate. *It can't be all bad*, you think as you put the strip in your mouth and swallow it.

"The green is designed to nourish your auxiliary brain," the Planet Leader explains with a smile.

"But I don't have an auxiliary brain," you say.

The Leader's face flushes a light blue as she realizes her mistake.

"Medic!" she calls. That is the last word you hear.

The End

You wait for someone to come help you. You do not know how many hours or days pass while you wait. But nobody ever comes.

The End

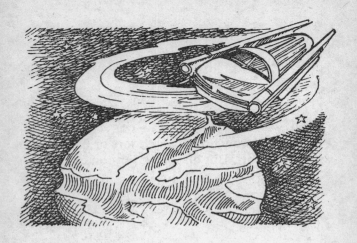

As you approach Galinka, the planet appears to be red with canal-like lines running over the surface.

"Those lines are the guidepaths for our ship," the Great Master explains. "We glide over the surface of the planet in the enclosed paths, then we enter the interior through various portals."

Soon the ship slips into one of the paths. At the end of it, gigantic doors slide open and the ship goes inside.

"Years ago we destroyed the surface of the planet by war. Ever since that time we have lived in the interior.

(continued on page 95)

"Now," continues the alien, "we must pay our respects to the Planet Leader."

Soon you are standing before the Planet Leader. She looks exactly like the Master except there is a clear crystal prism in the center of her forehead.

"This is an Earthling," the Great Master says when he introduces you.

You extend your arm to shake hands.

The Planet Leader gasps and then yells, "Imprison the Earthling immediately!"

If you go along quietly with the guard, turn to page 82.

If you protest this harsh decision, turn to page 110.

I don't think wolves can climb trees, you think. You run to the nearest tree and start to climb. The wolves are right behind you. You reach up and grab a branch, but before you can pull yourself up, a wolf bites you in the ankle.

Determined, you pull your body up into the tree. Beneath you, the wolves howl.

I'm safe, you think.

With the light of dawn, you make a horrifying discovery: your hands and feet have turned into furry paws.

The End

You sail north, trying always to keep land in sight. Finally, along the coast, you see one house, then another. Soon you see an entire town.

You see other ships anchored in the harbor and turn in that direction. Luckily, a pilot boat comes out to meet you. You call to it, explaining that you are not skilled enough a sailor to bring the ship into the harbor.

Soon fifteen people have scampered up the cargo nets onto the deck. When you are on land, a great celebration is held in your honor. It is a joyful day.

The End

"I am afraid to eat your food," you say. "It is not designed for my Earthling body."

"I suspect that is a wise decision," the Planet Leader says. "In that case, we shall have to take you to your home soon so that you can receive the kind of nourishment that your body requires."

You agree reluctantly. You would like to stay here longer, but you know that you cannot go without food.

"Thank you for your kindness," you say. "I shall never forget you."

The End

You swim frantically away from the serpent, but it continues to follow you. Then you have an idea. As the serpent swings its head at you and misses, you grab on to its neck, just behind the gills. The serpent tries to shake you off, but you cling tightly. It shakes and twists and wriggles. Still you hang on. You know you are safe as long as you can stay on its neck.

Finally the serpent tires of trying to rid itself of you and it swims out of the cave. At the last minute you slide off its neck.

You are glad to see that the green light shines brightly upward once more. Unwittingly, the serpent has solved the aliens' problem by opening up the entrance to the cave. Now the green light will once again guide them. You are proud to have accomplished your mission.

The End

Fantasia leads you quickly to her home. You are safe inside when you hear the long, ominous howl of a wolf. You are grateful that you listened to her.

Just as you are feeling calm and content, the house shakes; then it shakes again.

"Earthquake!" screams Fantasia.

Through the window you can see buildings sway and trees rock back and forth.

If you run to the window to watch the effects of the quake, turn to page 85.

If you grab Fantasia and pull her into the doorway with you until the shaking stops, turn to page 108.

Quickly you drop to the floor and sit on the rope.

The elevator door opens.

"The Earthling is still here," says one guard to another.

"Yes, but what happened to his covering?" says the other, staring at your bare legs.

In seconds the guards are inside the laser prison, pulling the rope out from under you.

Then they leave you alone. This time you know that there is no escape.

The End

You are standing only a foot away from the mutinous alien. As he turns toward the control panel, you smash your foot into his legs. Laser beams flash as the alien falls and the gun flies across the room.

Immediately the Great Master of the mother ship draws his gun. With one quick beam of light the traitor is immobilized. Then the Great Master turns to you.

"You are a hero," he says. "And now I am going to make you an offer that has never been extended to an Earthling before. If you wish, you may come with us and visit Galinka. Or, if you prefer, we will beam you back to your home."

If you want to go home now, you may end the story here.

The End

However, if you wish to visit Galinka, turn to page 94.

Frantic, you look around for a place to hide.
Now there are five pairs of red eyes looking at
you. They begin to move as they circle around
you. Closer and closer they come.

Suddenly you have an idea.

Turn to page 96.

The head lunges toward you, but you swim away. Then you break off a stalagmite. When the serpent comes near you again, you take the long piece of ice and wedge it into the serpent's mouth. It shakes its whole body frantically. Then it bumps into the diamond and a chip breaks off.

You grab the chip as it floats past you. Then you swim quickly through the opening and back to the saucer.

The aliens cheer when you enter. You have solved their problem without having to bring up the diamond. When the serpent broke the ice barrier the powerful green light was restored to its original intensity.

"For your reward," says the leader, "you may keep the chip. As long as you value it, you will be blessed with extraordinary powers of insight and strength. Guard it well. It is worth far more than all the gold in the cave. Now we will take you home."

The End

You look around. The fence of lasers is about six feet high. A pipe regulating the air pressure of the cell runs across the ceiling above your head.

You realize that your only way out is over the top of the lasers. You take off your jeans. Then, with the help of your pocket knife, you tear the pant legs into strips and tie them together.

Next, you tie a shoe to one end of the homemade rope and fling it over the pipe while holding on to the other end.

The shoe and rope fly over the pipe and come down on the other side. Then you tie the two ends together.

(continued on page 107)

You shinny up the double rope and begin to swing back and forth.

Suddenly you hear an elevator.

If you take one last swing, turn to page 90.

If you drop to the floor and hide your rope, turn to page 102.

You stand in the doorway as the entire house shakes. Chunks of the ceiling fall around you, but you and Fantasia are protected by the door frame.

When the earthquake is over, you run outside to see if you can be of help. You are grateful that you had the presence of mind to act wisely. It saved your lives.

The End

You turn around and begin to run. But the night has grown dark and the black shadows of the trees confuse you.

Frantic now, you try to think of what you should do. You look around for a weapon, but you cannot see in the dark.

The creature with the red eyes is gaining on you. You can feel its hot breath. Wildly, you swing your arms, hoping to scare it away. You scream when your hand touches the thick fur coat of the animal.

The End

"But what did I do?" you ask.

"You have insulted the Planet Leader by pointing your hand at her," the Master explains sadly. "The punishment for that is death."

"But on Earth shaking hands is a sign of courtesy and respect."

"You should have known it was different here."

"But how?"

"You should have made it your business to inquire about our customs."

"*You* should have made it your business to tell me," you say defiantly.

"The Earthling is right," the Planet Leader says. "Cancel my order and bring it some nourishment."

Soon colored strips that look like sticks of gum are presented to you with a grand gesture.

(continued on page 111)

"Please," says the Planet Leader. "Eat as much as you like."

If you eat the red strip, turn to page 78.

If you eat the green strip, turn to page 92.

If you refuse all nourishment, turn to page 99.

If you eat the black strip, turn to page 112.

The black strip smells like strawberries, so you don't mind eating it.

"This nourishment aids our ability to experience joy," the Planet Leader explains.

Soon you experience awesome happiness. In your memory you relive ordinary experiences and they seem wonderful. You think about your friends and feel a surge of warmth and happiness. You think about the fight you had with your parents but you feel love, not anger. A sunset you once saw comes into your mind as a visual feast of unsurpassed beauty. Everything you have said or done in your past takes on new meaning.

"I wish that I could have this with me always," you say to the Leader.

"As long as you cherish the memory, the experience will be yours," the Leader says.

"It is a great gift you have given me," you say. "When I return home, I shall never forget you."

"And that will be your gift to me," she says.

The End

American Morse Code

A	. _	N	_ .
B	_ . . .	O	. .
C	. . .	P	. . . . .
D	_ . .	Q	. . _ .
E	.	R	. . .
F	. _ .	S	. . .
G	_ _ .	T	_
H	. . . .	U	. . _
I	. .	V	. . . _
J	_ . _ .	W	. _ _
K	_ . _	X	. _ . .
L	___	Y	. . . .
M	_ _	Z	. . . .

HINTS:

$\wedge$ = T

☐• = N

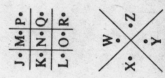

J•	M•	P•
K•	N•	Q•
L•	O•	R•

A	D	G
B	E	H
C	F	I

How to study the hints:

1) Look at the shape that stands for the letter *T*.

2) Find *T* in the code.

3) Figure out why $\rangle$ stands for *T*.

4) Look at the shape that stands for the letter *N*. Notice the dot.

5) Find *N* in the code.

6) If you can figure out why $\boxed{\,\cdot\,}$ stands for *N*, then you have cracked the code.

7) Translate the message.